LULU and the VERY BIG MEANIES

by Mac McGooshie
Illustrated by Alexis Hogwood

#1 of Lulubug's Week in the Life *series*

MUSLIM WRITERS

Muslim Writers Publishing
Raleigh, NC
2013

Mac McGooshie

Title: Lulu and the Very Big Meanies
Author: Mac McGooshie

ISBN: 978-0-9854638-2-3

Published by:

Muslim Writers Publishing
D MCNICHOL, LLC
Raleigh, NC

www.MuslimWritersPublishing.com

This work is fictional, and is not meant to depict any actual historical events, people or places.

Bismillah Ar-Rahman Ar-Raheem

Alhamdulillah for everything!

For Allah by way of the benefiting the Ummah, insha

Allah,

For Ahmed, my Mr. Awesomeness,

And for my own Lulubug,

the vanilla cream in her Mama's coffee.

Table of Contents

Acknowledgements

First and foremost, all thanks to Allah for his blessings and his making this book possible. The internet, it is a marvel. Jazakum Allahu khairun to my mini batch of testers, AKA Brooke and brood, for input and advice, to my Judy for her friendship till the cows came home, got comfortable, slept, took showers, had breakfast and went out again, to Widad for the platform, Lexi for her kitschy illos, and to Camilla for her eye for detail. And of course, jazakum Allahu khairun and thanks to my personality- and/or patience- filled family, y'all know who you are...

Mac McGooshie

Lulu
and the

VERY
BIG
MEANIES

By Mac McGooshie
Illustrations by Alexis Hogwood

All About Me

My name is Laila, but my friends call me Lou.
Mama calls me Lulu, and the neighbor calls me
Ladybug. Baba calls me Habibti, which means
"My Love," and sometimes he calls me "Habibi
Baba," which means "Daddy's Darling." Call me
what you'd like– just not late for supper, *insha
Allah*, because I love to eat!

My family and I are American Muslims. We
live in a small town in southern Virginia, where
there are a lot of farmland and churches all
around. We have some very nice people around
us, but not many Muslims. Our neighbors aren't
Muslims, and my Tutu and Poppop aren't
Muslims. Mama's sisters and brothers are
Christian, so they're not Muslims. Mama used to
be a Christian, too.

Not everyone likes Muslims around here, but
mostly, people put up with us. Mama says the
media give Muslims a bum rap. I believe that,
because I don't think I'm an evil person. Mama
and Baba aren't evil, either, even when Mama is

yelling at me to pick up the towels off the floor, put my clothes away, clean up my bedroom or stop eating the cookies she bought for school lunches.

(To be fair, she didn't hide the cookies very well. MOST people put stuff where it won't be found. FYI, or For Your Information, inside the entertainment center is not a great place to hide cookies, even if your kid doesn't watch baby videos anymore. Your kid will find it. Better to hide cookies in the Chores Jar. I mean really. Who would look in the Chores Jar?)

Baba has a restaurant where he makes the BEST PIZZA IN THE WORLD. I can say that because it's true. Baba is a most excellent cook and pizza man. I love him especially much because he gives me anything I want. Almost anything. Unless it's *haram*, (which means "not allowed") or "too old for me" or Mama says no, if I want it, Baba does his best to get it for me. And I have my ways of getting around the Mama restrictions.

Baba is an Egyptian American. I've been to Egypt once, so I got to meet all my uncles and aunts and cousins on Baba's side. They are so nice to me. Mama says that's "Arab hospitality," and not to start acting like a spoiled princess, because it's not becoming– becoming *what*, she won't tell me, ha ha. She also says that when they make their way to our home, we need to be sure to show them the same hospitality, because our *deen*, or religion, requires it. No problems there, as far as I'm concerned. My Baba's family are all kinds of nice.

Even Uncle Abdel Fatihah, the Cairo taxi driver, is super cool, even if he *does* drive like a maniac. I love him like a maniac. There are not many people in this world that surprise Mama, but Uncle sure does. When he was young, he had an accident and lost his left arm. That wasn't what surprised Mama (though I'd never met anyone who was missing an arm, and I thought *that* was unusual). When we first came to Egypt, he and Baba's sister, Amitoo Wafaa, came to pick us up at the airport. Uncle's car is a tiny little Italian car, with a stick shift and a small trunk. We wondered how in the world a man who was missing an arm could drive a stick shift, but he picked us up at the airport, so maybe Amitoo Wafaa helped him? No. He drove and shifted by himself, driving through Cairo like the rest of the crazy taxi drivers. And Cairo doesn't have any stop lights! Mama was so scared. Plus, we kept on hearing someone honking at us. It turns out, it was actually Uncle honking at everyone else, that is, while he wasn't steering and shifting. Oh, and talking on the cell phone to Uncle Mohamed, my Sitoo, Baba's Auntie Fatima and Cousin Hameda. Amitoo Wafaa held the phone up to his ear every time the phone rang.

Mama loves Uncle Abdel Fatihah very much, but won't let him drive me anywhere. I guess that's for the best, but it *was* a fun ride.

Baba and Mama got married about a hundred years ago and had three kids. I'm the youngest–Mohamed and Shawky, or Mo and Sho, as I call them, are my twin brothers. They aren't *quite* as good in school as I am, but they are awesome soccer players and they give me whatever I want, just like Baba does. Therefore, they are acceptable to me. Baba taught them that it is *sadaqa* to be kind to little sisters. Plus, I've got skills and I'm not afraid to use them. I can make their lives a living you-know-what if they aren't nice to me. Let's just say that I *have* pushed *that* envelope. My brothers are tall for twelve-year-olds, Mama says. They haven't even hit their "growth spurt" yet, but they look just like two matching pimply giants to me.

What can I say about Mama? Mama is the cranky one in the house, but she has her good moments. Once in a while Baba gives her a little kiss on the cheek and she actually smiles! Mama makes sure we pray, eat, get to school on time, have clean clothes and gets us to our soccer games. She's not a great cook like Baba, but heck, who is? She does make the best cheery pie in the whole world, though. (Cheery pie is kind of like cherry pie, only better, and especially *ala mode*, which means with ice cream on top. Trust me. Much better.)

Mama calls herself a part-time lawyer, but she doesn't do very much legal work at all. She says that's because she's too busy taking care of us. As if! If she stayed busy all the time, she'd clean our bedrooms and clean the bathroom floor. Instead, she tells us to clean our own rooms and says things like *"presumption of culpability"* and *"de facto disaster area."*

I brace myself when Mama starts talking fancy because that means a storm is brewing in her head, and I don't dare move. I told her once that I had to run for shelter because she was going to start one of her long windstorms. The details of that incident are ugly. Let's just say I never made that mistake again.

As for me, I am tall for my age, too, which is nine. I skipped a grade because Mama made me—she said I needed to be *challenged*. What that actually means is more homework and reading.

Tricky how something that sounds like it should be a pretty good deal, because it's one year less of school, is actually a bit of a bummer sometimes.

On the bright side, Baba thinks skipping a grade will look good on my record for when I want to go to med school. "Eyes on the prize, Habibti," he tells me, "eyes on the prize." I try to remember that when I have to read an extra boring book. Mama says *sabr* should be one of my personal *jihads*. I agree in theory, but I just don't have the patience. Mama shakes her head when I tell her that, because "sabr" means "patience." Baba laughs so hard *every time* I say that. He laughs a lot for a grown man, and *alhamdulillah*, I'm so glad for that. Baba is a fun guy.

My best friend Toni is ten and in fourth grade just like me. Toni is not a Muslim, but she's been my best friend since we were babies. Now that I'm in her class, though, she's "redefining and placing restrictions on our relationship." That's what Mama calls it. I call it being bossy. She doesn't want me to laugh in class, raise my hand too much, or tell her fart jokes any more. I understand that she's just trying to help me fit in, but gosh! School's hard enough. We have to find fun where we can get it, ya know?

The good thing is, Toni changes back to her regular old self after school. We have a lovely time once we're back home. We jump on the trampoline and roller skate on the driveway. We also pick on her little brother Spencer a lot– it's just so easy to do. Once in a while, their mom, Miss Abigail, invites me over for dinner when they're having *kosher*, or *halal* hot dogs. *Good stuff, Baba Ganoogie.*

Sometimes Mama invites Toni over for dinner, too. This usually happens when my brothers are at my cousins' house. (Mama says she's worried about my ability to socialize, or some crazy something like that! I socialize just fine. I think Mama just misses cleaning up after Mo and Sho.)

This weekend, though, Mo and Sho will be home and it's supposed to be business as usual.

MAMA SAY NO BOYS

Thursday after school Mama called me into the kitchen. *Oh no*, I thought, *if she's just starting with me now, it's going to be a very long night.* I took a deep breath and braced for the windstorm. So much for a video chat with my cousins today.

"Come sit down for a second."

Uh oh, it must be pretty bad if she's asking me to sit down, I thought. "What's wrong, Mama?" I asked, thinking that alhamdulillah, she wasn't mad at me, but she *was* mad at *something.* "Can I get you a glass of water?"

"No, thank you. I would like to talk to you about school, though." After I nodded my head extra seriously-like, she said, "Your brothers came to me yesterday to tell me about what's been going on in school."

"A lot of things go on in school, Mama. Mo and Sho don't do anything wrong, though. So what's the problem?" I asked and started tapping the kitchen table. I was feeling protective of my twin brothers. I have a special soft spot for them on Thursdays because on Wednesdays, they buy me ice cream on the way home from school.

Mama gave me the raised eyebrow and said, "No, they didn't do anything, but I was a little concerned with their school dance. It's supposed to be a mixed gathering..."

I didn't know what Mama wanted to talk to *me* about– I wasn't the one who was planning the school dance. I was ready to bolt. "Okay, Mama, I will take that information under advisement."

"Whoa, whoa, there girlfriend. Sit." Saying "girlfriend" was Mama's way of trying to sound like a young person. She wasn't very good at it, but I wasn't about to tell her that. "I was wondering whether you have any girl-boy activities in school that I should know about."

"Of course not, Mama, and if there were, you'd be the first to know," I nodded slowly again to show how serious I was. *Gosh, those middle schoolers will ruin it for the rest of us*, I thought.

Mama was pretty serious when it came to girl-boy activities. She was dead set against them unless it was for some academic reason, because boys and girls aren't supposed to be friendly, or "familiar" when they get older. That means, no boyfriends when I get older, and dating is definitely haram.

I've known about that since I was a baby, though, because Baba says I used to run around saying, "*La ilaha il-Allah! Mohammed ar-Rasoul Allah! Mama say no boys! Mama say no boys!*" I think I was very cute when I said that.

Toni, though, wasn't worried about no boys. She was worried about one boy. She had a crush on Joshua, Miss Patty's son. Joshua is two years older than I am, and a year older than Toni. She thinks he's cute, even though it looks like Miss Patty paid the gardener to do his hair. Joshua is also missing some of his teeth. I hope he gets them back some day, but I'm doubtful.

Toni is always worried about what Joshua thinks. I try not to hurt Toni's feelings, but I am a little upset that she likes him so much. No boys. That's what Mama says, and I think that this time, Mama is right. Boys make you stupid–even Miss Abigail and Miss Patty said that, and they should know, because they each have a boy. And Mama has two.

Anyway, Mama seemed to go off in her own little world, and I snuck out of the kitchen. At least when she's busy thinking about something, she cooks good food. It looked like chicken and dumplings, with extra carrots on the side. Maybe it would be a good night after all. The *azhan* for *asr* prayer started and I went to make *wudu*. Baba was coming home soon, and we could all pray together, insha Allah.

We Are NOT Happy Campers

I thought that Baba coming home early from work would calm Mama down, but I thought wrong. After asr, she told me to go upstairs and do my homework, scolded Mo and Sho for no reason, then asked Baba to come in the kitchen to "talk." Usually, I try to distract Baba with my cuteness, but Mama was on a roll. She closed the swinging door so she could "get some privacy." Hmmph. Didn't she know that I have my ways of finding things out?

This time, though, I did my homework like Mama said, and then I took my binoculars out to look at the birds in the woods. I had a feeling something major big was going to happen, like when Baba bought the new car. I would like a new car, as a matter of fact – a fast silver sports car, insha Allah, just like Mama wants. That would be totally acceptable.

By 6:30, I was getting hungry, so I made the dinner table as much as I could without going into the kitchen. I started to clang around a bit, so the parent-people would take the hint. A few minutes later, they came out of the kitchen with a big pot of chicken and dumplings and bowls. *Good stuff, Baba Ganoogie.*

We sat down to eat, and everyone said *"Bismillah Ar-Rahman Ar-Raheem"* like we always do. That means "In the name of Allah, the Most Gracious, the Most Merciful." Baba says we have to say that because it's good to do a good thing in Allah's name.

If we walk down the street, we say, "Bismillah." When we lie down or get up, we say, "Bismillah." When we go out to play, we say "Bismillah." For almost everything, we say, "Bismillah." I never get tired of saying "Bismillah." I hope Allah never gets tired of hearing it.

Sometimes we say other *duaas* too. A duaa is a little extra prayer when we want to ask Allah for something. I am learning some Arabic duuas little by little from my Amitoo Wafaa.

Baba brought up the dance at the dinner table. *Uh oh.* "So what's going on with the school dance?"

"Nothing," said Mo. "We already told Mom we're not planning on going."

"You're right you're not," said Baba. I've never heard Baba sound strict before, but there it was, all laid out at the head of the table. "Your mother has been telling me what else has been going on. You've been getting phone calls from girls?"

"Shawky did, Dad, not me. He got off the phone fast, though."

"Yeah, Dad. One girl. She wanted a homework assignment, and then she asked me to ask her to the dance." *Oh snap*, I thought. *Someone is gonna get it!*

"And you told her what?"

"That I wasn't going. That's it. I hung up real soon after that. *No worries, mate!*" Sho said in his best Aussie accent. He is simply splendid! I love him crazy sometimes, almost as much as I love myself.

"Okay, then. What about you, Mo? No girls hanging on you at school?"

"Only about fifteen, Dad. Nothing I can't handle. And I don't let them call the house and upset Mom," he answered. I wasn't sure if Mo was joking or not, but Mama's eyebrow raised, and Baba rubbed his forehead like he had a headache.

"Apologize to your mother, boy," Baba said, and Mo did. Then things smoothed out, and I let the conversation turn to me.

"You know what, Baba? I got another A in Science. Ms. Matthews thinks I should enter the science fair next year to get the practice for when I'm older."

"*Masha Allah*, Habibti! Very good! How about Math?" It was good to see Baba think about something nice for change.

"Baba! I aced it! You should be so proud of me!" Getting an A on homework was probably not worth all the excitement, but hey, I love my Baba to be happy, and he is happy when he is talking about me and my good grades.

"Habibti! I'm so happy for that! And your *Quran* lesson?"

"Oh. Not quite as good..." It was hard to get excited about that.

"Why? What's wrong?"

"Oh Baba. It's just hard to learn online with Amitoo Wafaa."

"*Ma'alish*, Habibti. I will practice with you later tonight, insha Allah. Every time you practice the Quran, it is a good deed, even when it is hard for you," Baba said.

"*Especially* when it's hard for you," Mama said.

"*No worries, mate*," said Aussie Sho.

"*Jolly good, luv!*" said British Mo.

My brothers are awesome! That's what I thought before Mama let the hammer hit.

"Your Baba and I think we're going to have to consider some big changes around here," she said.

"Like what, Mom?" asked Sho. "We didn't do anything wrong." Sho was right. But that didn't stop Mama from going off the deep end.

"No, you didn't. But since everyone is getting older, there are more things that can affect your deen, and your father and I are very concerned about what's going on in school."

"But Mom, we have no problem staying away from girls, and we'll keep Lulu away from boys," Mo pleaded.

"Yeah," I answered. "My brothers will keep the boys off of me like swatting mosquitoes." I started slapping my arms like my backyard in August.

"That is not the only thing your Baba and I are worried about. First, there is really too little for you to do here in this small town. Better to go where there is more available, and be in a place where there are more Muslims around you. Plus, you really should be getting a more thorough education. I'm concerned with a few of the local teachers. Some are really good, but there are a couple that I just don't want you to have anything to do with. That high school history teacher is a little scary to me, and I'm not entirely convinced of the curriculum anyway. Your PE teacher is *way* too pro-Second Amendment, and the home-ec teacher gives off a definite Stepford wife vibe."

Before I could ask what any of that means or start having a temper tantrum, Baba said, "No ifs, ands or buts about it."

Very, Very Crummy

I was NOT in a good mood when I went to school on Friday. It didn't help that the two meanest people on the planet started giving me grief for no reason. Very B. and Very C., the Veries, as I call them, are Veronica Batchelor and Veronica Crumb. They are two miserable people, that's for sure, and they're only happy when the people around them, including yours truly, are miserable, too.

The Veries are tattletales, too. At the beginning of the school year, they ratted me out to the teacher. Roberta, the shortest girl in the whole fourth grade, couldn't see the projector screen in the auditorium, and so I let her sit on my shoulders. Everything was fine until I tried to stand up (it was a science experiment in gravitational pull), and Robbie fell and knocked her head on Miranda's. CLUNK! Very loud, as a matter of fact, but it sounded worse than it actually was, really. What's a little head bump between friends? But sheesh! The Veries were bent on making a scene, and Ms. Matthews sent me and Robbie to the office to have a "little talking to." I called it a victimless crime, because Miranda thought it was kind of funny once she stopped seeing stars, but Ms. Hooper, or "Hoops," as I like to call her when she's not listening, found no humor in it at all.

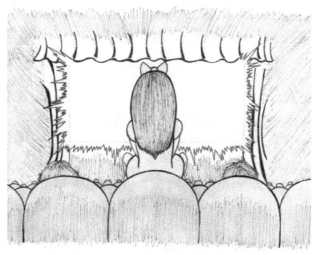

That was the beginning of my fourth grade school year. If Hoops hadn't known what a treasure and delight I usually am, on account of kindergarten, first and second grade, she would have made my fourth grade very unpleasant– her words, not mine. The Veries have tried a lot to get me in trouble since.

When those two started in on me in Social Studies, I was in the mood for a throw-down. I tried extra hard to be good, though, because I didn't want to give Mama any more reason to move away. Plus, it was Friday, and that was the Muslims' day. On Friday, Muslims pray at the *masjid* for *Jumaah* prayer. Baba goes to Danton by himself sometimes, and sometimes he takes Mama. During the summer, he takes all of us, and we usually go out for lunch, too. *Good times.*

Very B. plopped down at the table where I was eating my lunch and asked where my brain was. I told her mine was where it was supposed to be, and she should stop sitting on hers, and then told her to go pound dirt. Robbie and Miranda started laughing like crazy when I said that, and Very B. went back to her miserable little corner. Then Very C. came up behind me and pulled my shirt up. On instinct, I swung my arm back and smacked her in the face. Hitting her in the face was by accident, I promise! Very C. went crying to the office and came back dragging Hoops a few minutes later. I was very angry, but I held it together. I was very impressed with myself.

"Hello Hoo-, Ms. Hooper," I said in my most charming voice. "What can I do for you?"

"Hello, Laila," Hoops said in her all- business voice. "Veronica here tells me that you smacked her in the face. What do you have to say?"

"Purely accidental, Ms. Hooper," I answered. "She pulled up my shirt in the back, and I was just trying to protect myself. If you don't believe me, I will take a lie detector test." Then I turned to Very C. and asked, "Did you tell Ms. Hooper that you pulled up my shirt first and opened my back to the world?"

"Well that was an accident too." Very C. lied. I would let it go just for today, but not without giving her my very mean stare.

"Okay then, it appears that we've had a misunderstanding," Hoops said. "Veronica and Laila, will we have any more misunderstandings today?" I think that's what they call a *rhetorical question*, because if Hoops got called again to the lunch room, I know for a fact that she would not be happy.

Very C. gave me a nasty look, and said, "No, Ms. Hooper." I shook my head and Ms. Hooper left.

"Next time, it won't be an accident," I said. "Don't touch me again." Then I growled like a German shepherd.

Very C. jumped back like she was scared.

Mission accomplished.

Just the Facts, Ma'am

By the time I came home from school, Mama went from normal human drill sergeant to high performance clean machine. She had already started throwing things out, which was crazy, because some of that stuff was probably mine! The trash cans on the side of the house were too full to put the lids on properly, so I dropped my book bag and went to investigate. I started pulling bags out of the cans. One bag was filled with empty food boxes and breakfast cereal bags for recycling. Looks like Mama cleaned out the kitchen while I was at school. Wasting is haram and Mama hates to waste. She probably took the food from the boxes to the woods in the back to feed the squirrels and the birds like she usually does. I made a "mental note," as Ms. Matthews calls it, to check out the woods with the binoculars from my bedroom window. Those birds were awfully mean when it came to their food, even when they were supposed to share. The squirrels were going to get pecked, no doubt about it.

Another trash bag was filled with Mo's and Sho's old sneakers. *No problem. Not mine. Acceptable.* The third bag was filled with stuff that Mama had always wanted to get rid of, but Baba said no. Baba was a pack rat, and liked to keep the darnedest stuff. One time, Baba got mad when Mama tried to throw out a case that used to have tools in it. Baba bought the tool case new for Mama when Mo and Sho were babies. She said it was the best thing he'd ever gotten her. (Yeah, I know "tools" sounds like a crazy "best gift ever" because a kitten is certainly not a tool! But as Poppop says, there's no accounting for taste, and Mama has always been a little odd.)

Anyway, Mama loved her toolset, that is, until the day that Baba started taking tools to work with him. First it was a Phillip's head screw driver, then the hammer was gone. Then it was the ratchet set, and another tool, and another, until all that was left was the set of Allen wrenches, which, it turns out, are just a bunch of funny-shaped L's. Mama tried to throw the case away after that, since after so many years it was old and beat up and empty, but Baba said it could be used for a million other things. I used it as my surgery kit for a while, but when Mo and Sho found out I had their tools from their work bench, I couldn't play surgeon any more.

There was a lot of stuff that Baba said he couldn't live without, but he never touched them. A lot of those things were in the trash now. *Adios.*

Phew. From the looks of the trash, Mama hadn't touched my stuff yet, and there was still time to protect my domain. I picked up my book bag and ran into the house. "Asalaam alaikum! Your room's next!" Mama yelled as I ran up the stairs.

"Not if I have anything to say about it!" I screamed, completely forgetting to answer her greeting. *Oh, that's not good*, I thought, *she's really gonna get me for that!* "Wa alaikun asalaam!" I found an empty pad of paper and started writing down everything I have, starting at my dressing table. That way I would know if she was trying any funny business, like she did with Baba's stuff.

I was counting the window curtains when I noticed something in the woods that definitely wasn't killer birds. Maybe it was a deer. Whatever it was, it disappeared down the hill before I could get my binoculars.

Sometimes deer wander around our back yard, and if I'm quiet, I can observe them. Once, I saw that they were there during *fajr*, or dawn, and it was still very dark, so Baba let me use his night vision goggles after we prayed. The deer were eating all the cucumbers and tomatoes from the garden, but Baba said to go ahead and let them, because it is sadaqa to feed the animals. Ka-ching! Another good deed to make Allah happy, insha Allah!

I went back to my inventory, but Mama came into the room and told me to go outside to play with Toni if I had no homework to do. For once, she wanted me to play, and for once I didn't want to go! But I pick my battles, so I gave Mama a kiss on the cheek, said "salaam," and went to find Toni.

Toni came to school late because she was getting a cavity filled, so I didn't have a chance to talk to her about moving. She would be at least as devastated, which means "super sad," as I was, for sure. She was practicing her clarinet when I came over, and Spencer answered the door with a mouthful of potato chips. Spencer yelled at Toni over the squeaky clarinet, so I could see every disgusting piece of chip in his mouth. "Toni! Laila's here! She wants to play! Hurry up and get down here!" Leave it to Spencer to annoy me even when he's trying to be helpful. Mama says that once boys turn ten years old, they turn gross, and stay like that at least until they're forty. Spencer was only six, but he is gross enough for me. Let's just say he's an early achiever.

"Thanks Spence. By the way, didn't your mother ever teach you not to yell with your mouth stuffed full of potato chips? That's pretty disgusting, man."

Spencer laughed like an evil genius. "That's just the look I was going for." He stuck out his tongue and showed me more chips. It was gross.

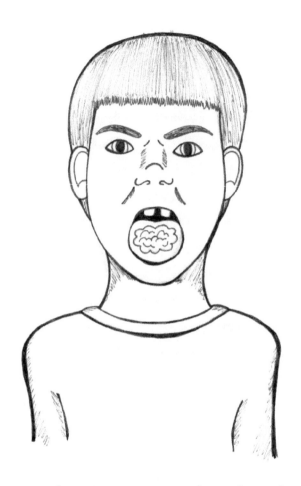

Just then, Toni came out from the parlor, which is a fancy word for family room, and she smacked Spencer in the arm. "Spence, Mama told you not to talk with food coming out of your mouth. Fly straight, or I'm gonna tell Dad." Spencer looked at Toni a little annoyed-like, and then Toni and I went outside and sat on her stoop.

"Okay, Toni, you're never gonna guess my news. It's huge. HUGE."

"Cool. Y'all getting the new car? You've been promising that thing for almost a year now, and I have to tell you, Lou, I'm having my doubts about you ever getting a sports car. Maybe by the time you're old enough to drive, your daddy will get you one," Toni said.

"Okay, okay, I get it, you're disappointed. No. Look. This is way worse." I shook my head and held my breath for dramatic effect. "We're going to be moving out of Martinsburg."

"Oh, okay," Toni said, like it was nothin' but a thing. This was not the reaction I was expecting. As a matter of fact, I was expecting screaming and crying, and I was a little disappointed. I stepped up my game a bit for more drama.

"My mom is throwing stuff out right and left, so by the time we move, there won't be anything left but the clothes on our backs and what we can carry in a Grocer's Haven bag."

"I think that might be just a *slight* exaggeration. No way your mom would throw *everything* out," Toni said. She was always skeptical– I don't know why.

"Are you kidding? She'd probably throw Mo and Sho out, except it's against the law!"

"OK, Lou, let's think this through a minute. You're going to move? When's that gonna happen?"

"I don't know yet."

"Where are you gonna move to?"

"I don't know yet."

"Are you gonna go to a different school?"

"I don't know yet. No wait. Definitely, I'm gonna go to a new school."

"Oh, well, okay. When are you gonna find out about the rest of the details?"

"I don't know yet. Maybe we should ask my mom."

"Yes, that would seem to be the logical thing to do. You wanna ask now?" Toni was pretty smart. I should have done that last night, instead of trying to make Baba feel bad and acting like a baby. So Toni and I went into my house and hunted Mama down.

"Miss Bennie! Miss Bennie! Are you here?"

"Hello, Toni, how are you today?" Mama always answered Toni very politely. She likes Toni a lot– sometimes more than she likes me, I think. That's because Toni uses good Southern manners.

"Very well, ma'am, and I hope you are," Toni answered. "My mama says 'hi,' by the way. She really liked the trifle you sent home the other day, she just hasn't had a chance to thank you properly yet." What was this—a love fest? Get to the important questions already! I nudged Toni's arm. I *only* nudged it, but Toni said, "Ow!"

"Laila," Mama said in a warning voice. Then like honey, "Toni, what can I do for you, sweetie?"

"Miss Bennie, Laila says that you're going to move soon. Is that true?"

"Well, yes it is, Toni. I'm not sure when that will be, but sometime after the school year's over."

"Where are you moving, if you don't mind me asking, ma'am?"

"It'll be either Danton or Riverside, depending upon where we can get Laila and the boys in a new school."

"Why are you moving? We are surely going to miss you!" Toni said, her eyes starting to get a little wet.

"We'll miss you, too, sweetie, and you can come and visit any time!" Mama didn't tell Toni why we were moving. I think because she didn't want her to feel bad. Alhamdulillah, Toni stopped asking Mama questions then, because I was about to start crying again, too.

Moby

April showers bring May flowers! And it was
POURING on Saturday, so no soccer games,
hooray! After breakfast, Mama told me to clean
out my dresser drawers and closet. I had to put
all my small clothes into a bag to take to the
thrift store. No prob. I like cleaning out my
drawers– it makes room for new clothes. I am a
fashionista big time! I have a whole bunch of
scarves that match with every dress, shirt, skirt
and pair of pants that I own. My shoes match my
bags, and I even have a beach bag that matches
my flip flops. I am stylin', if I may say so myself.

Mo and Sho cleaned out their small clothes,
too. Of course, they don't take care of their
clothes as nicely as I do, so I'm sure their clothes
don't bring as much money. Today, though, they
had three large bags. Baba said that they might
make more money for sheer volume.

Mo and Sho packed the SUV, which was full
of stuff from Mama's cleaning windstorm, and
there wasn't even room for me! Mama said she
would tie me to the luggage rack on top of the

SUV, but then changed her mind when she saw me climbing up. "I was joking, Habibti. Come on down," she said.

"But Mama, this will be a great ride. I will be the only person ever in history to ride on top of an SUV in the rain. I will put it in my memoires, so my children can read about my adventure," I said. Well, apparently, Mama is not so concerned about her grandchildren's reading materials, because she ordered me down right away and made me get in the back seat.

Mama usually lets me look through the racks at the thrift store in case there is a jacket or sweater with great style that I cannot live without, but not today. As soon as the bags and boxes were dropped off, we headed for home. I used the time in the SUV to ask Mama about moving. Our best conversations were usually in the car, while she had her hands on the steering wheel.

"So what do you think?" This was our usual "special talks" starter, when we wanted to talk about something serious, like when my grandfather died or when my parents wanted me to skip a grade.

"About what, Habibti?"

"About moving, Mama. I don't want to move. Not at all." I was serious and not crying. Unlike Baba, Mama didn't like crying, except in "certain circumstances," and in my long nine years of life, I still don't know what that means.

"I know, Lulubug. But it is for the best, insha Allah."

"Why? We are good Muslims whether we stay in Martinsburg or go to a big city," I said, most logically and calmly.

Logic usually works on Mama, but not today. "Alhamdulillah, we try to be good Muslims, don't we? But you need other Muslims besides your family around you. You need Muslim friends, and you need, we all need, to be part of a Muslim community."

"Speak for yourself, Mama," I said with just a little too much sassy-pants. Mama's eyebrow shot up, and I said sorry right away. Being a smart mouth was not respectful to my mother. I needed Mama to be happy with me, not only so I could get to *Jannah*, but because, as my Uncle Patrick says, you catch more flies with honey than with vinegar. Not that Mama is a fly, but she sure does like honey. And sweet talk.

"Habibti, you'll make new friends, insha Allah, and you'll love your new school," Mama said with her eyebrow down again. Then she turned on the right turn signal which was opposite of our house.

"Do you even know where that is? Because I think you forgot where our house is!" *Uh oh, sassy-pants in that, too*, but Mama laughed.

"Let's take a road trip, Habibti. We'll visit the school I want you and your brothers to attend." I nodded my head even though Saturdays are not for school, as far as I am concerned. I like road trips.

Mama and I like to go to Riverside because of the great shopping opportunities, but this time, we didn't stop at a mall. We went to the Riverside masjid instead. There were about a hundred people there, and all the women were wearing a scarf, like Mama. Some of the girls were also wearing a scarf, and some were wearing long dresses. There were some boys that looked like Mo and Sho's age, and they were playing basketball. No way I would ask to play with these boys. Mama would *kill* me– twice!– no joke. They were probably not even as nice as my brothers anyway.

We started snooping around a little bit, but Mama doesn't like that word. We found the woman's prayer area upstairs, which was beautiful! We took off our shoes and of course, said "Bismillah" as we went into the room, . There were fuzzy, soft green carpet strips and fancy schmancy lights called *chandeliers*. There were some fold-up chairs and a book case full of Qurans in Arabic and in English. I fell in love with that room, and I hope that my house will be big and peaceful like that when I grow up, insha Allah.

We found the school, which was on the third floor of the masjid. It was too white and too clean. "I don't like it," I told Mama.

"It looks like a very nice place, Lulubug. What's wrong with it?"

"Smells funny."

"I think it smells nice! That's just disinfectant."

"If I go to school here, I think I shall be sick every day."

"I think you will be just fine, insha Allah."

"I think you are wrong."

"Hmm." Mama gave me an eyebrow and that was the end of that. Sometimes Mama is a woman of few words.

We walked down the hall a little bit and then we heard a BANG! and then BAM! A girl about my age ran into me and knocked me on my bum! I was too surprised to cry, but man, did that hurt! Mama helped me up while the girl said, "I'm so sorry! So, so sorry! Forgive me, insha Allah."

I said, "What's your problem?" I was angry because my bum was sore, and I'd probably have a big bruise.

"Look. I said I'm sorry. Move on," said the girl in a snip. Already I didn't like the school, and I wasn't going to like the people at school apparently, either. Mama raised her eyebrow at the girl, and the girl looked down and apologized again. "I'm sorry. I should have been paying better attention. I'm looking for my big brothers, who are supposed to be up here working on their geography projects. My mom wants to go home soon, so she asked me to find them."

"Okay, then, where is their classroom? We'll help you look," Mama said.

"Just down here," the girl said, and pointed behind her. "Thank you, sister, I'm sure I can find them by myself." *Did she just call my mother "sister"?*

"Well then, asalaam alaikum... wait just a sec. You go to this school?" Mama asked.

"Yes," the rude-polite girl answered.

"What grade are you in?"

"Fourth grade, sister."

"Excellent, masha Allah. What is your name?"

"Laila, but my friends call me-"

Just then, two identical pimply faced boys, who were NOT my brothers, came out of one of the classrooms, and one of the boys yelled, "Hey Moby!" I think they were talking to the new Laila, but what a very strange nickname- just like the Great White Whale! Nicknames are not supposed to be mean, so I didn't understand why her brothers were calling her a whale. She didn't look anything like a whale-- not even like a porpoise.

Laila turned around and yelled to the boys, "I'll be there in a minute! Mom's looking for you two!" Then she looked at me and said, "Well, you know my name, so what's yours?"

I answered, "I'm Laila, too. But my nickname is Lulu, and my friends call me Lou. You can call me what you'd like," I invited politely. Then I said, because I was so curious, "Why are you named after a whale?"

Laila laughed and said, "My nickname is after my grandmother's name, Maybellene. We call her 'Grandma May,' which is why no one calls me "May." No one calls me "Laila," either, because I have three cousins named Laila, and this school is full of Lailas. So somewhere, sometime, someone started calling me Moby. The Quran says that no one should call anyone by bad nickname. 'Moby' is not a bad nickname at all, and it's unique, just like me. Therefore, it is acceptable." Mama smiled at that, I have no idea why. I have to admit, though, I like the way Moby thinks. "Moby" *is* unique, and if, Allah forbid, I end up going to this school, I want an acceptable and unique nickname, too. "Twister" is good, I think.

Moby ended up being pretty nice. She showed us around the school, upstairs and down. The younger grades were on the first floor, and the rest of the grades were upstairs. The principal's office and the front office were also on the first floor, next to the men's prayer area, or *musalla.* After she showed us around, Moby said she had to go to her mother. But first, she gave me her messenger address and said "asalaam alaikum." Maybe it would not be the most terrible thing to go to school here.

Baba, the Hero

Usually on Sundays, Baba didn't work at the restaurant– I got him all to myself! Well, not really, I had to share him with my brothers and Mama. I let him take Mo and Sho to the basketball court after fajr prayer and then let him have coffee with Mama. I was being a very nice person to share Baba, I thought, until Baba said he wanted to go house hunting.

"Baba, you're not going house hunting. That's it. You're going to spend the whole day with me," I said. I would never use that tone with Mama, but Baba liked it when I ordered him around, I think. He liked to feel needed.

"But you can come with me."

"But I don't want to."

"But we need to find a house."

"No we don't."

"Yes we do."

Okay, this wasn't going the way I thought it would. Maybe I had to try a different approach. "Baba, I thought you loved me."

"Of course I love you. You are Habibi Baba! But we still need a house." I made my eyes get wet with tears. I wiggled my lower lip, so Baba would see that I was seriously sad, but Baba smiled. "Oh Habibti, we need a place to live when we move to Riverside. So don't cry. Let's go find a house, and insha Allah we can find one for you with a nice bedroom."

At least Baba was thinking about me. It would be a good idea for me to have some input on the new house. It would be terrible if I ended up sleeping in a cold, moldy dungeon. I need something on the second floor so I can watch the birds, like I do now. Mo and Sho can have the dungeon.

Baba and I don't talk well in the car like Mama and I do, because I can't give him my special hug. "Why do we have to move, ya Baba? It's making me sad, and I don't like it! I'm going to miss all my friends, and my teachers, and the woods out back. You know my day isn't complete unless I can watch the birds."

"Aww, Habibti," Baba said, "you know there are birds in North Carolina, too. And you can keep your friends and talk with them every day, if you want. It's very easy on the computer– you do it all the time!"

"Not the same thing, Baba," I said. "I'll miss them. I don't know how I'm going to recover from such a shock to my psyche." Baba laughed at that, but I was being very serious. I'm not quite sure what a "shock to the psyche" is, but I think it has to do with how people feel bad when they're put in a new and terrible situation.

"Habibti, you'll do fine, insha Allah. You jumped from second grade to fourth grade, and I know you were a little bit upset that you weren't going to school with your same friends every day, but masha Allah, you did just fine. You adjusted to the schoolwork, all your friends like you, and so does your teacher."

"Not the same thing," I repeated. Hmm. I would have to think of a new argument very soon.

"You know, Habibti, we are not the only people to move in order to be good Muslims."

"You're not going into a speech about all the suffering in the world are you?" I groaned. Usually Mama was the one. Baba glanced at me and grinned.

"Our Prophet Mohamed, *sallallahu alaihi wa salaam*, and the first Muslims moved to Madinah so that they could establish Islam and be good Muslims. But alhamdulillah, there is already a place close to us where we can practice our deen and become better Muslims, insha Allah. We don't have to move to Madinah."

I was not convinced. "But Baba, we're Muslims, and we're allowed to pray anywhere in the world!"

"That is true, Habibti, very good!" Baba smiled his big happy smile, then put his arm in front of me and hit the brakes HARD. Alhamdulillah, there was no one following, or they might have run into us!

Why did Baba stop? Because there was a kitten in the middle of the road! Baba pulled the car over to the side, next to a big cardboard box and put on the blinking lights. Then he picked up the kitten from the road before another car could hit it. He looked in the box and waved for me to get out of the car.

Turns out that box was full of kittens! Instead of happy, Baba was angry. "Habibti, this is a bad thing that people do. Their cats have kittens, or dogs have puppies, and they leave them in a box on the side of the road, where the animals can get hit so easily by a car. Allah forbid someone tries to avoid hitting one of these animals and gets in an accident because of it."

"But they're so cute! Can we keep them?" I asked.

"No, we cannot keep six kittens. We'll take them to the shelter and have them taken care of. Insha Allah, all of them will have good homes. We'd better head back to the house and let your mama take care of these." *Mama takes care of kittens? Since when?* Baba put the box of kittens on the back seat and shut the door, and let me sit in the back so I could keep an eye on them. While I was wondering how to talk Mama into letting me keep the kittens, they scooted and scratched around the box. One of the kittens was laying very still and crying, and looked a little disgusting even though he was cute. I left him alone except to put a shop rag over him so he could stay warm. One of the little guys tried to jump out of the box, and I petted him. He didn't seem scared of me, and I was so happy for that!

Cat People

When we got back to the house, Mama was showing Mo and Sho how to remove wallpaper. Alhamdulillah, I'm glad Baba and I dodged *that* bullet! Mama wasn't too happy when she saw the box of kittens, but she made a list for Baba and sent him to the drug store so she could take care of them. This was going to be interesting.

"Baba, can we stay here and play with the kittens?" I asked.

"I still need to go house hunting, Habibti," Baba answered, "but you can stay here and help your mother with them." Mama gave him a look out of the corner of her eyes.

"Thank you Baba! They're so cute! Can we keep them?"

"Absolutely not," Mama butted in. "We are not keeping a box of kittens, and we can't keep everything your Baba brings home." It turns out that Baba has brought home boxes of animals since he and Mama got married– kittens, puppies, rabbits, and even turtles! He brought home some cockatiels when I was a baby and Mama took care of them for six months until she found them a good home. I wish I'd known that,

- 45 -

on account of I love to watch birds with my binoculars.

Anyway, Mama looked at each kitten, at their ears and mouths and bellies, including the little sick one. Mama said that they were all about six weeks old and all needed to eat and have a good flea bath. The sick one, we'd have to take to the vet the next day. We wouldn't give that little guy a bath until the vet said "okay," but we would try to keep him very warm and try to feed him so he could gain some strength, insha Allah. Mama would dab a little bit of flea soap water on the kitten to try and kill some of those fleas.

After we fed the kittens some kitten formula (which is fake mama cat's milk) and soft kitten food, Mama put each one in the new kitty litter box. She showed me how to gently take a kitten's paw and scratch at the litter. This teaches the kitten how to use litter to cover its messes, like it should know how to do by instinct. Well, there were more pleasant things to do with kittens, but if I was going to try to talk Mama into letting me keep them, I'd better show her that I could take care of them.

After litter box duty, Mama put me, Mo and Sho on flea bath duty. Mo washed the kittens very gently with the flea soap and warm water. *Subhan Allah*, kittens look very disgusting when they're wet! Sho dried each kitten with one shop towel and Mama's blow dryer on low, then wrapped it up in another towel and gave it to me. My job was to keep each kitten warm and to soothe it while it got sleepy. Kittens can't make enough heat on their own, so it does them good to have a warm body to get cozy on. Alhamdulillah, two of the kittens fell asleep inside my shirt right away, and I snuggled them next to each other in a clean cardboard box that was lined with old newspapers.

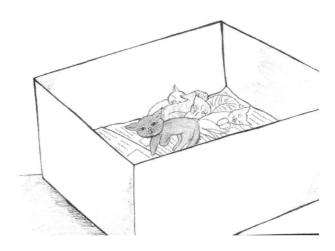

When the clean kittens were asleep, Mama told us we all did a good job, but she was crying! "The sick little kitten died a few minutes ago. *Inna lillahi wa inna lillahi rajioon,*" Mama said. "Let's make duaa for it, and for us, and for the other kittens." So all four of us put our palms up and closed our eyes and said a little prayer.

After that, Mama made us lunch while Mo and Sho dug a little grave in the woods and buried the kitten. I sat at the table in the kitchen and asked Mama if she was still sad, because I certainly was.

"I am a little sad, Habibiti, but things happen for a reason, and I can't know why Allah makes everything happen. It was the kitten's time, and there is nothing I could have done to make the time any later. Does that make sense?"

"No, Mama, I don't understand. It was just a little kitten, why did it have to die?" I started to cry and Mama led me to the living room couch and let me lie on her lap while she brushed my hair back with her hands. That felt very nice.

"Oh, Habibti. Allah is the best planner. Our religion requires us to take that as truth. So let's think on that for a minute. I know it's hard, but let's do it. How was the kitten when you first saw her?"

"It was a 'her'?" That made me cry even more.

"It's okay, baby," Mama said. "Was she sick?"

"I think so, she seemed sick."

"Was she in pain?"

"I think so, Mama. Because she was squeaking and crying," I said, remembering how pitiful she sounded in the car.

"She was. And I couldn't get her to eat anything. She was too weak and too sick to eat."

"But maybe if we got her to the vet sooner..." I started crying some more.

"Ah, baby, you cannot say that. Only Allah tells us when life begins and ends," Mama said quietly. "And Allah is the one to give us blessings. How many kittens were there altogether?"

"Six."

"And how many are there now?"

"Five."

"How do the five look?"

"Oh, Mama, they're so cute. And they're clean, and they ate good, alhamdulillah."

"Alhamdulillah. You see? Could you appreciate how healthy the kittens are if you didn't know how sick the other one was?"

"I guess not," I sniffed. "Mama..."

"Yes, baby."

"Can we keep the kittens?"

"No."

"Can we keep *one* kitten?"

"Ask your Baba."

"Thank you, Mama."

Alhamdulillah, that definitely meant "Yes."

Something Strange Afoot

Mama made me take a shower before *zhur* prayer because I smelled like the kittens *before* their flea baths. I sniffed inside my shirt, and she was right– I was ripe! After my shower, I wrapped myself up in Mama's fuzzy bathrobe and wrapped my hair like a turban, like Mama does. I always feel so grown up and cozy when I do that. Mama scolds me when I strut around the house in her bathrobe, saying she doesn't want me to trip over myself, but I know she's trying not to laugh because she can't even keep her eyebrow up.

I sat on the bed, combing my hair and looking out the window when I saw something in the woods. It didn't look like a deer this time, but I couldn't tell for sure. By the time I got my binoculars, it was gone. This was going to take some serious investigation. Nothing, and I mean NOTHING, gets to be in my woods without me knowing about it. But the zhur azhan called, and the investigation would have to wait.

*'Allahu Akbar, Allahu Akbar, Allahu Akbar, Allahu
Akbar,
Ash hadu la ilaha illAllah, ash hadu la ilaha illAllah,
Ash hadu an-na Mohamedar rasoul Allah, Ash hadu an-
na Mohamedar rasoul Allah,
Hayya 'alas-salah, hayya 'alas-salah,
Hayya 'alal-falah, hayya 'alal-falah
Allahu Akbar, Allahu Akbar,
La ilaha illAllah.'*

That means:

Allah is Greatest, Allah is Greatest, Allah is
Greatest, Allah is Greatest,
I bear witness that there is no god except Allah, I
bear witness that there is no god except Allah,
I bear witness that Mohamed is the messenger of
Allah. I bear witness that Mohamed is the
messenger of Allah,
Hurry to the prayer, hurry to the prayer,
Hurry to the success, hurry to the success,
Allah is Greatest, Allah is Greatest,
There is no god except Allah!

I love to hear the azhan playing. Mama has a free computer program that lets us know when it is time to pray. The recording of the azhan was from a nice man in Saudi Arabia who gave away his voice for the program for free. The software makers gave way their azhan program for free too, because it is a sadaqa to remind people to pray. Ka-ching for them!

Sho led the prayer for us, and Mama and I prayed behind my brothers. I had a hard time concentrating on my prayer because of whatever was going on in my woods, but I tried. After we prayed, I made duaa for the kittens and my Tutu and Poppop.

After zhur, I sat at the kitchen table, about to put on my sneakers, but Mama stopped me right away. "You're not going anywhere, girlfriend. You have homework to do, kittens to take care of, and a bedroom to clean. And I want you to stay clean for school tomorrow."

"But Mama, I won't get dirty, I have no homework, the kittens are sleeping, and my bedroom is already clean," I said. Before I even finished my sentence, I knew I had a loser argument, because the cutie brown kitten had made it out of the box and was stalking Mama's foot. Mama picked up the kitten and handed him to me before she picked up the second one, a cutie orange that made it out of the box and was sniffing the space between the stove and the cabinets. Probably chasing an ant. A good hunter, insha Allah.

"First of all, Lulu, your bedroom is never clean, and second, these kittens are going to need some care." Mama always had something to say about my bedroom. There is a reason my bedroom is arranged the way it is, and she has just never been able to see my organizational genius. But anyway, I would have to take care of the kittens to prove to Mama that I was capable of keeping one forever. Already she had given me a list of things that would have to be done to take care of it. Fresh food, fresh water, clean food dishes, litter box, clipping its claws, keeping it warm, brushing it when it sheds, cleaning its vomit and hairballs, giving it flea medicine. That was a lot of stuff, but I was up to the challenge. The mystery in the woods would have to wait till Monday.

Baba came home after *isha*, which means it was already dark and I was getting ready for bed. Within seven seconds (a personal best), I talked him into letting me keep a kitten, alhamdulillah! Baba is so sweet. I told him about taking care of the kittens and then told him about what was going on in the woods.

"Did you ask your brothers if it was them?" Baba asked.

"They were inside when I saw, Baba. Mo was in the shower, and Sho was about to go into the shower. No, this was something different—maybe even Sasquatch!" I knew I was letting my imagination get away from me, but the drama was good, and Baba always liked a good story.

"Really now," he said. I don't think he bought it this time, but he never disappointed me. "One day after school this week, I'll come home from work in the afternoon and we'll check things out, insha Allah. Okay?"

I gave him a hug and a kiss, and his prickly cheek kissed me back with a lot of scratches. "You're the best, Baba!"

Monday Morning Blues

The school bus was late, which was a little inconvenient because of the monsoon that was happening in southern Virginia on Monday morning. Alhamdulillah, Miss Abigail drove us to the bus stop and let us wait in the minivan.

"Hey, Ladybug," Miss Abigail said and looked at me in the rear view mirror, "Toni tells me that you're going to be moving soon. I'll tell you, I'll be sorry to see y'all go. You and Toni have been friends for your whole lives, and no one makes a better dessert than your mama."

"She does make good desserts," I answered, not really excited to talk about moving, and not even wanting to talk about the kittens. Usually, I love to talk to Miss Abigail. She is a very nice lady. She is so nice, in fact, that I have a hard time understanding how such a great lady can have such a gross little boy. Spencer was sitting in the front seat with his mouth closed and his hands on his lap because Miss Abigail found him playing with a smooshed banana in a most disgusting way while he was in the back seat. As

I said before, he is an early achiever in all things gross. He should get a trophy. I never want to eat a banana again. I hope he doesn't ruin the rest of the fruits for me.

The rain was pounding on Miss Abigail's minivan and thunder was rumbling like roller skates. I made a special silent duaa so we wouldn't have to move. Baba says that the heavens open up when it is storming, and it is one of the best times to make duaa. I wasn't going to waste it on small talk, even if Miss Abigail is one of my favorite people, and even if Mama does make some killer desserts. Toni had her eyes closed and wasn't up for talking either. She hates to wake up in the morning, especially on Mondays.

After a while, Miss Abigail got a phone call from the school saying that Mr. Eddy, the bus driver, had crashed, but he wasn't hurt, alhamdulillah. Miss Abigail made some phone calls and then drove us to school, but not before stopping by Very C.'s house. Oh brother. She was going to pick up the Veries, and I was going to be stuck in the minivan with them!

"Miss Abigail, those Veronicas are very mean to me every day. Can we leave them here?" I asked.

"No, sweetie, I'm going to take them school as a favor to Ms. Crumb. They can sit in the back. You don't have to talk to them, and you don't have to like them. You just have to get along while you're in my vee-hicle," she said in my favorite Southern accent as she popped the hatchback for them to drop their book bags.

Very B. kneed me in the shoulder on her way to the back seat, and Very C. hit me in the head. Miss Abigail saw Very C. and scolded her. I could feel the Veries' eyes burning a hole in my head when Miss Abigail did that. No problem. Mama would call that "vindication" in her lawyer-talk. Miss Abigail put on some country music and headed to the school.

At school, the Veries smiled at me as they grabbed their bags and ran into the building, but not with nice smiles. More like they wanted to vomit on me, and then rub it into my clothes. Toni and I ran into school together and made sure Spencer got to class okay. We made plans to have lunch with Robbie and Miranda. I would tell her about the kittens then, insha Allah.

Ms. Matthews smiled at us as we came into the classroom. Half the class was empty, and the students who were there were reading "All Summer in a Day," a story from the Language Arts book. The Veries were staring into their books like they were staring at the moon. They were up to something. I sat down and reached into my book bag, and felt something strange. It was wet, a little slimy, and felt a little thicker than water. Was I bleeding? I found my book and pulled it out, and my hand and the book were blue! My book bag was ruined! My notebooks! My pencil bag! Everything was covered in blue, and the book bag was messy and leaking on the floor. "Ms. Matthews! Something happened to my book bag!"

It took me a split second to realize that the Veries were behind this, but they didn't move their eyes from the books. They were smiling their real sickening smiles. Toni and the rest of the class couldn't keep their eyes off my blue mess. Toni got up to help me, but Ms. Matthews asked her to sit down. She came over with a trash can and paper towels and asked, "What did you do? Is this another experiment? Laila!"

"No, Ms. Matthews! Why would I experiment with my book bag?"

"Well, that's an awfully big pen to leak all over the bag. Are you carrying an inkwell with you?"

"I don't even use blue pens, Ms. Matthews," I said. "You can ask my mother." Mama buys only black writing pens because they are always acceptable in the business world, and blue is not always acceptable. She is a stickler for black pens.

"We will get this cleaned up and figure out what happened. Don't worry, okay?" Ms. Matthews was very kind and smiled at me, like she always does. She gave me paper towels to wipe my hands and pulled the trash can close. I wondered if Ms. Matthews would get ka-ching! sadaqa like Muslims do, and wished that she would become a Muslim because I loved her so much.

"Okay, Ms. Matthews, I'll try not to be too upset. But I must warn you now. My heart is broken, because I love my book bag and everything in it," I said.

"Fair enough," Ms. Matthews answered as she got up to hit the button to the front office and asked for the janitor to come right away.

Alhamdulillah, the janitor knew just how to take care of the ink mess, like he did it a hundred times before. He put the book bag carefully into a trash bag, and carried it down to the office with me, where Ms. Scarry, the school secretary took me to the bathroom to wash my ugly, ugly blue hands. Hoops was waiting in the office for me, with blue powdered gloves and butcher paper laid out on the floor. Mr. Pivens, the vice principal, was there, too. We sat on the floor around the book bag, which was sitting in the trash bag, which was sitting on top of the butcher paper. Hoops asked, "Laila, can you tell me what happened?"

"I reached into my book bag and out came the blue," I answered.

"Did you put anything in your book bag that would have caused this?" Ms. Hoops asked very carefully. She sounded like Mama when she was using lawyer words.

"No ma'am. I don't own anything that would cause this. I don't use blue pens, my markers are in a hard case, and they are washable anyway, and I don't play with my mother's eye makeup," I answered. "Not anymore."

"Okay then, let's take a look," Hoops said and passed me a pair of gloves. She took each thing out of the book bag, stated what it was for Mr. Pivens to write down on his clipboard, handed it to me, and I laid it on the paper. My whole life was in that book bag– my school life, anyway. Two text books, my binder, workbooks, calculator, and pencil pouch. Also, my lanyard with my house keys and my cell phone case and my journal and my lunch box. All ruined.

"Ms. Hooper, this makes me sad. And angry," I said, getting more upset by the minute. "This is my life. And I know I'm not supposed to blame people without witnesses, but I think–"

"Hold on right there, Laila. We have something here." Hoops held up a zippered sandwich baggie, covered with wet and dry blue ink.

"I've never seen it. I promise!" I said. Was I going to get framed for busting my own bag? That would be so unfair!

"No, no, we're not jumping to conclusions. First I'd like to call your parents, okay?" Hoops said. *Oh snap!* I was going to be in trouble no matter what. Hoops took me to a seat in the office where I waited for Mama.

The Wrath of Mama

Surprise, surprise, Mama did not kill me on the spot. Probably because there were too many witnesses. She looked around the front office, gave me a kiss, and checked the ink on my hand. Hoops waved Mama into her office and immediately closed the door behind her. Fifteen minutes later, Mama opened the door and asked me to come in. Mama said, "Ms. Hooper was just telling me what happened to you. I'm going to ask you one time. Did you put the ink in your book bag?"

I shook my head and said, "No, Mama, I didn't."

"Do you own ink like this?" I shook my head. "Do your brothers own ink like this?"

"Not that I know of, Mama. And Mo and Sho wouldn't do that to me. They are very nice big brothers, in the grand scheme of things," I said.

"You're right, Habibti, they are," Mama agreed. "Well, tell me how you think this happened. Because this is not acceptable, and we need to get to the bottom of it." Mama paused, "Who had–?"

"Mama, I know who did it, just I can't prove it because I don't have any witnesses," I said, interrupting Mama. "The only people who came near my book bag since Friday besides my family are Toni, Spence, and the Veries, when we were in Miss Abigail's minivan today. Toni wouldn't do that to me, and Spence was too busy smooshing bananas and getting scolded by Miss Abigail. The Veries put their book bags in the back with mine when Miss Abigail picked them up this morning. Plus, they were acting suspiciously when we took our book bags out, and also in the classroom."

"The Veries? These are the girls who have made a habit of picking on my daughter since she started the fourth grade?" Mama asked Hoops.

"Ah, well. The Veries, as the kids call them, tend to be, um, less well mannered than they should be. Laila, in fact, had a minor brush with one of the girls on Friday. It wasn't enough to warrant a call home, and I think Laila acted appropriately, including threatening her with a growl," Hoops answered. *She saw that?*

"That was Very C., Mama. Very B. tried to start trouble with me before Very C. did, but I sent her packing," I said, getting more angry by the minute. "You know, it's not fair. I don't ever do anything to them. No one does anything to them, but they are always so mean, especially to the little kids."

"Okay, baby, let the adults take care of this now, insha Allah," Mama said. "Why don't you go sit outside for a little bit? Mama and Ms. Hoops, er, Ms. Hooper, will talk for a few more minutes, and then I'll take you home."

Mama knows how to take care of business.

I asked Mama what she and Hoops talked about after I left the room, but she told me it was adult business. "But Mama, what's going to happen to the Veries? There are no witnesses to the crime." Muslims cannot convict people of a crime when there are no witnesses. I had no witnesses, even though I knew those two meanies were the ones.

"Oh, there are witnesses, Habibti. The ones who did it are witnesses. So is Allah, *subhanna wa ta'ala.*"

"So what are you going to do?" I asked, really curious. Mama was being secretive, and a little bit scary.

"Well, first, Habibti, I'm going to talk to your father, and ask your brothers if they had anything to do with this. I don't think that they did– it's just not their style," Mama said matter-of-factly. "Then, assuming that the boys had nothing to do with it, I'm going to talk to Miss Abigail, and then I will probably have a little talk with Veronica Crumb's mother, and maybe Veronica Batchelor's mother, too." *Oh snap. Mama was going to sue!*

"I didn't know that you knew them, Mama. Do you think you can get a lot of money?"

"Huh? What? Oh, no, I'm not going to sue anybody, Habibti, at least I don't think I will," Mama smiled. "We need to take care of business, though, so this doesn't happen again. Not to you, and not to any other child, insha Allah." I smiled, too. Didn't I say that Mama knows how to do that?

We stopped at Baba's restaurant, and he let me wash my hands with his gritty soap, which changed my hands from blue to zombie gray. It would be a while before all the ink was gone, but alhamdulillah, Baba told me that permanent ink was not as permanent on hands as a person might think. I could live with zombie hands for a while, no problem.

Baba made me baked spaghetti with cheese on top and Mama didn't even make me eat veggies on the side like she usually does. They let me watch cartoons while they talked in the restaurant kitchen for a while, then they came to sit with me. Mama had her own plate of pasta, with vegetables and chicken and garlic, which was a little bit stinky, but I didn't care. Seeing Mama on a mission was a beautiful thing, especially if the mission was for me. Garlic breath was nothin' but a thing.

When we got home, Mama turned on her computer and asked me to take care of the kittens, which were running around crazy in the kitchen. No prob. Alhamdulillah, they were cuter than they were the day before, and didn't even make a mess on the floor! I mixed some formula into their food and put it on a plate for them, and they waddled over and started chowing down like it was the last food on earth. The fastest kitten, Cutie Brown, climbed on top of the food plate like he owned it. The other Cuties tried to climb on the plate, too, and pushed him off. They were all so adorable, and I didn't think that I would be able to choose just one when it came time for them to go.

Mama called me about twenty minutes later to come to the computer. Mama wouldn't let me put my real name online anywhere, because she wanted me to be safe. But she found the Veries online, even their pictures! And, she found the blue ink that Very B. and Very C."liked" very much.

"Mama, why would the Veries admit that they like something that is probably going to get them in trouble?" I asked.

"I don't know, Habibti. Sometimes people aren't so bright, and I guess that especially applies to bully types. I mean, think about this. Does being a bully make people like you more?"

I did think about it, and said, "No, nobody really likes the Veries, even though they don't pick on everybody in class– just me and Robbie. I think they pick on me because I'm the youngest, and they pick on Robbie because she's the shortest."

"Do they get anything *tangible*, that is, something they can touch, by being bullies?"

I thought about that, too. I remember that last year they took lunch boxes from two kids in the first grade, and stepped on their sandwiches before throwing the lunch boxes back at them. The Veries didn't get anything from that, except in trouble. Hoops was on them like white on rice, as Uncle Patrick says. "No, I don't think so."

"So does it make any kind of sense that the two Veronicas choose to act like bullies?"

"No, I don't think so," I said, shaking my head carefully so Mama could see that I was listening very hard.

"So, can those two girls be considered smart?"

"Definitely not, Mama. They are not the sharpest tools in the shed, are they?" Uncle Patrick taught me the "sharpest tool in the shed" saying, and it was my favorite. I *loved* being able to use it in an everyday conversation.

"No, I don't think they are, Habibti. Now go make sure the kittens are using the litter box properly."

When Mo and Sho came home, Mama grilled them about my backpack and the ink. Mama didn't think they had anything to do with my disaster at school, but she wanted to make sure. I think Mo was ready to cry by the time Mama was done with them, and Sho was so upset, his voice got high like an opera singer. I hugged my brothers because the Veries ended up giving them a rough day like they did to me, without even trying. When Sho saw my hands, he squeaked, "Subhan Allah, Lulu! No wonder Mom is upset. Who would do that to you?"

"The Veries did it, we are almost 100% sure, Sho, but we need to prove it," I said, and filled my brothers in on what happened from start to finish.

The boys were silent for a minute, and then British Mo said, "*Jolly good, let's prove it, luv!*" My ears perked up like a puppy dog's, because Mo always had a great plan, and Sho was always good on the details. Did I mention that I love my brothers because they are awesome?

The Bee's Knees

On Tuesday, I went to school with my bag lunch, a spiral notebook and pencil, and nothin' else but my pride, as Uncle Patrick says. (Uncle Patrick is full of cool things to say. Mama says that one of these days, she's going to make him stop talking to me.) I felt a little bit naked and much lighter without my book bag. I missed it.

The sun was out, beautiful and warm. Everything was green and shiny wet, and the sky was extra blue– no clouds at all. The azaleas were out, too. Subhan Allah! They are just too gorgeous to be sad. It would be a fabulous day, even if I had to be in the same room with the Veries for part of it. Toni and Spence were at the bus stop, and were huddled up with Joshua. I almost felt bad that they were ignoring me, but it was such a pretty day, and I had bigger fish to fry (thank you, Uncle Patrick). When Mr. Eddy came by in a new-old school bus, I got on board and sat by myself. I tried to look sad, and I was, only a little bit.

That was the loneliest day of school I ever had, but I got through it. Ms. Matthews gave me two new textbooks and three workbooks, which I carried around to look like I was suffering. I am good at drama, I must admit. Just to make the Veries remember me, I gave them a very sickening smile, and a "shaka brah" with my gray zombie hand. The Veries turned a little gray, too, ha ha.

(Tutu tells me that in Hawaii, the locals say "shaka, brah!" to each other, and hold their hand up with their pinky and thumb out, and the middle three fingers down. I'm not sure exactly what "shaka" means– something like "Hey, whassup?" "Brah" means "brother," but you don't really have to be talking to your brother. Surfers like to use the "shaka" sign when they're going into the water. I think it means that they're not afraid of sharks, but don't quote me on that.)

When I got home from school, Mama said "Asalaam alaikum" and marched me into the kitchen to take care of the kittens– except there were only three left! "What happened? Where are they?" I screamed. "Mama! Please don't tell me that they died! Please, Mama, please! I can't take any more bad news!"

"It's okay, Lulubug, calm down. They're all fine. I found homes for two of them, though. The two orange cats, a boy and a girl, are going to the same farm just outside of town. Insha Allah, they'll be barn cats once they're big enough, and they'll get rid of the mice and rats who are eating the farm animals' food. They'll have a good home, and run around a lot in the sunshine."

I had to think about that for a minute. When I was in Egypt, I didn't meet anyone with house pets. There were a lot of cats in Egypt, though. Their lives were not easy, unlike American pets. They had to work for anything they ate. Cairo had some big rats and mice– bigger than the kittens! Once in the middle of the night, Mama woke up and saw a huge rat on the outside of the bedroom window screen, and we were on the fourth floor! I was so glad I slept through that, and alhamdulillah, I was happy the window screen was so strong. And I felt sorry for any cat that had to attack *that* for its supper. (I can imagine Cutie Brown saying, "Meow? Are you kidding me? Meow?") But as Baba says, Allah is the one to give sustenance, and if there were lots of cats in Egypt, that meant there was a lot of food, too.

"Okay, Mama, that is acceptable," I decided.

"Alhamdulillah," Mama answered. "Now, why don't you get busy feeding the kittens and then make wudu, because Baba is on his way home."

I had almost forgotten that Baba and I were going to check out the funny business that was going on in my woods. After we prayed, I buttoned my sleeves and shirt all the way up, put on my explorer hat, and pulled my socks over my pants. Baba was doing the same thing and we put on our shoes together. We said "Bismillah," I picked up my binoculars, and we headed out.

"Masha Allah, Habibti, it is a beautiful day," Baba said.

"I know, Baba, that is the same exact thing I said this morning," I answered.

Baba and I both stopped dead in our tracks when we heard some banging. I couldn't see anything with my binoculars– the noise was coming from down the hill towards the creek. I passed the binoculars to Baba and let him look. Baba couldn't see anything either.

"Okay, Habibti, stay close and be quiet," Baba said as we walked towards the drop-off.

"Okay, Baba," I whispered, avoiding anything with three leaf clusters, because that could be poison ivy. When Baba stopped at the edge of the hill, I stopped. We looked down and saw some people at the creek, about a hundred feet away from our property line. I looked with the binoculars, but I couldn't tell what in the world was going on. There was a small pick-up truck backed up to the men. The men were working on the boxes, but they weren't banging any more. I couldn't tell what they were doing! I handed the binoculars back to Baba, and he knew what was going on right away. He knew the men who were working, too.

"Ah, Habibti, they're bees! They're building beehives! And those men are Nana Grable's sons, Bobby and Joel," Baba said. Nana was our neighbor further down the street. "Let's get a little closer and see what they're doing." Baba loved bees, and Mama's favorite *surah* in the whole Quran was "An-Nahl," or "The Bees." I wasn't that fond of bees, though, since I got stung by one when I was four. I stepped on it. Mama took out the stinger and put baking soda on my foot, but that didn't help the pain to go away.

"I don't want to, Baba. The bees might sting me," I said.

"Aww, Habibti, insha Allah, you won't get stung, and you're covered all except your hands and your face. It looks like there are no bees there yet anyway. But we'll stay far enough away just in case– just don't wave your arms or make any bees angry, okay?"

"I will stay back here, Baba, but you can talk to Mr. Bobby and Mr. Joel where ever you please.

Leave me out of it," I answered him, with a big dose of sassy-pants.

Baba laughed and headed towards the beehives. When the men saw Baba, they waved and walked towards him, handing him one of those hats with the net over it. He tried to wave me down, but I wasn't moving, no matter what. Baba talked to the men for a few minutes, checked out the boxes, gave them their hat back, and walked up the hill to me. As we headed back to the house, I started asking questions, but Baba told me I'd have to wait because he was out of breath from climbing the hill.

At the house, Baba told us that Nana's sons were building homes for bees on the other side of the woods, and the bees were coming from Florida. Bees are needed to pollinate the crops on the farms around Martinsburg, but every year, there are fewer and fewer bees. Bees around Martinsburg, and all over the country, are dying off, but no one is sure exactly why. Scientists think that it is probably many reasons combined. So farmers are bringing bees in from where ever they can get them, trying to establish them close enough to their farms to pollinate their crops.

Mama quoted the verses from the Quran:

And your Lord inspired to the bee, "Take for yourself among the mountains, houses, and among the trees and that which they construct. Then eat from all the fruits and follow the ways of your Lord laid down." There emerges from their bellies a drink, varying in colors, in which there is healing for people. Indeed in that is a sign for a people who give thought. (Quran, 16:68, 69)

Right then and there, Mama, Baba and I made duaa for the bees. Humans cannot live without them.

Mama asked me to go online to learn more about bees. I am still a little bit scared of them. (Who wouldn't bee? Ha ha!) But I understand how important they are, and not just to make Mama's tea sweet!

During the summer, a beehive may have as many as eighty thousand bees, but there is only one queen bee. The queen bee lays abut two thousand eggs every day during the warm months. Subhan Allah! A queen bee can live up to about three years, but other honeybees live only a few months. The drone bees are males, and they don't do the hard work. They have bigger eyes than other bees and no stinger.

When the weather gets cold, the worker bees kick them out of the hive, and they die.

The worker bees are the female bees, but they don't lay eggs. They do all the hard work of the hive. They clean it, they take care of the queen, they make the wax that builds the hive. When they want to make honey, they fly out of the hive and collect nectar from flowers. While they are flying from flower to flower, they pick up pollen from some and drop them off at others. One really, really amazing thing about worker bees is that they flap their wings very, very fast to act as an air conditioner to keep their hive cool during the hot summer. They also use their wings to "dance," which is a way of telling other bees where to go to find the good flowers. Bee wings flap over eleven thousand times per minute! That's what a person hears when he or she hears a bee buzzing.

I experimented by flapping my arms at full speed for one whole minute. Boy my arms were tired! I wondered if bees ever took naps, but couldn't find that information online. I imagine that they don't, because otherwise, where would the expression "busy as a bee" come from? Anyway, I couldn't flap my arms faster than one hundred flaps a minute. Too bad for me, that is not enough flapping to fly.

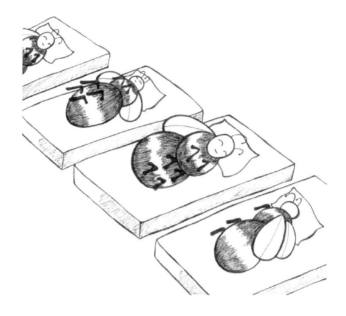

Each worker bee only makes a little bit of honey in her lifetime, and it takes ten thousand bees to make a pound of honey. Those bees have to go to two million flowers to collect enough nectar for that honey. That's a lot of flowers.

Humans have used honey and beeswax for thousands of years. Honey is used for medicine as well as for food. Beeswax has been used for medicine in the past, and also for candles, of course! Honey and wax have been used for makeup and hair treatments, too. The queen of ancient Egypt, Cleopatra, used to take baths of milk and honey so she could have beautiful skin.

Subhan Allah, the only thing more incredible to me than bees right then were the kittens, who were scratching around the kitchen floor, just begging to be played with. How was it possible that those little cutie-cuties could become even more cutie-cutier since I started studying bees?

Leaving the Sting to the Bees

On Wednesday morning, I was late for the school bus. I yelled for Mr. Eddy to stop as he pulled around the corner towards Center Street. Alhamdulillah, he heard me! I ran for the bus and he let me on. This morning, Toni and Spence were sitting together in the back, and Joshua was sitting between the two Veries in the back row. I bet Toni was just a little upset about that. I had no one to sit with, again, and Toni wouldn't look my way. Miranda and Robbie sat next to each other and they were in the back, too. There was no room for me. Day Two of our plan was officially in operation.

The Veries gave me their sickening smiles for a second when I got on the bus– I bet they would have been happy if I missed it. For now though, they were busy talking to Joshua a mile a minute. He didn't look disgusted by girls like he usually does. *Good old toothless Joshua. Miss Patty has a good egg there. Toni too*, I thought.

"Spence, get up so I can sit next to Toni," I said, with gusto.

Spence shifted like he was going to get up, but Toni said, "Spence, stay right where you are. Laila, go sit up there. Leave Spencer alone." My jawed almost hit the floor. Well, not literally, but it was close. The Veries started laughing like evil hyenas, and I gave them a mean look.

"I'm not doing anything to Spencer, Antonia Hammond. If you're going to be so rude, you can just be that way. I don't want to sit with you anyway," I said.

"Okay, Blue Hand Luke, I mean, Blue Hand Puke, beat it," Toni said. The Veries started howling then, and everyone on the bus was looking at Toni and me like they were expecting us to start throwing punches.

"Fine!" I yelled, and Mr. Eddy told me to sit down and face forward, and not to make him stop the bus. For the rest of the trip, Toni and the Veries chatted, and Spencer stared at me like I was from a different planet.

I was using my mother's bag to carry my books, and the Veries kicked at it as I picked it up to get off the bus. I stuck my tongue at them, and then bumped Toni like I was looking for a fight. She bumped me back, and the Veries thought that was great.

When I got to class, Very C. tried to trip me. I gave her the zombie shaka hand, though I wanted to smack her. Toni and Very B. laughed when Very C. stuck her foot out, and just for a second, I wanted to yell at all of them, but I didn't. I just gave them a mean look.

Lunchtime was lonely again. The Veries, Toni and Joshua all sat in the Veries' corner. Miranda and Robbie sat with some fifth graders, and I was by myself again. Gosh, if I had to do this for the rest of my school career, I may as well move to Riverside without complaining. Or home school with Mama, who promises I would graduate high school, and also visit the world by the time I was fourteen. *But I don't want to go to college as a fourteen year old! Everyone would pick on me because I'm the youngest for sure! Plus, I don't want to live in a dorm room, and I don't even drive! So I think that wouldn't be possible.... unless Mama would drive me to classes every day... how terrible would that be?...*

I shook my head, said "*audhu billah min shaytan ar-rajeem*" to get all those terrible thoughts of college out of my head, and started thinking about the Veries. Mo and Sho's plan was pretty simple– make Toni and Joshua pretend to be my enemies, and let them think that Toni wanted to prank Robbie. It turns out that the Veries think that Joshua is cute. (For the life of me, I cannot figure out why, but as Poppop says...)

Mo and Sho asked him to be nice to them for a couple days. The Veries didn't like Robbie and would be happy to make an evil plan with Toni and Joshua. The Veries would be caught in the act, while admitting that they were the ones who put the ink in my bag.

Perfect plan, right? All except for one thing. I didn't feel so good about it. It sounded like a good idea to start. But when it came down it, the plan was based on a big lie, or rather, a big bunch of little lies. Allah does not like lying. And Joshua is a boy, and Mama says "No boys!" For Joshua, my Mama would say "No girls!" especially not the Veries, who were very yucky girls. Not even as a favor to my brothers.

Plus, someone could accidentally get hurt, just so I could get a confession and my revenge. I would feel terrible if something happened to Robbie or Toni, just because they were trying to be good friends to me.

So, even though I didn't like the Veries, and even though they were mean to me every day, and even though they put the ink in my bag and ruined all my stuff, and even though I was worried that they might do more bad things to other kids, and even though my friends and my awesome big brothers were doing all of this for me, I had to stop the plan. Allah would take care of it for me.

Subhan Allah. This is what Mama would call "a life lesson in the jihad of sabr." And she would be proud that I figured this one out by myself. And Baba would be proud, too, and probably would buy me something very nice. And Mo and Sho would agree with me after they thought about it for a few minutes, and they would learn a life lesson, too, insha Allah.

I had to move fast if I was going to let everyone know that the plan was cancelled. Secret agents say "Abort the mission!" all the time when they get in trouble, and so that was my new plan. Alhamdulillah, people can only stand so much of the Veries. Joshua left their table and went back to hang out with the boys. I left the lunch room and waited for Toni in the bathroom on the opposite side of the school. A couple minutes later, Toni came into the bathroom and looked for my feet under the stall doors.

"Lou, are you in here?" Toni asked. "Hurry up, I only have a few minutes before they hunt me down. They are so needy! They're worse than Spencer after a shower when he's forgotten to grab a towel."

I laughed and came out of the last stall and washed my gray hands. Toni was hilarious. "Okay, Toni, you know what? I think we have to abort our mission," I said. "Can we just stop it?"

"Why? What's wrong? They're awfully close to confessing, Lou. Give me another day–" Toni said, looking in the bathroom mirror. She was so confident, and I loved her so much. I was tempted, but said no.

"Thank you Toni, but I am afraid you and Robbie are going to get hurt, and I don't like the lying. You don't like them, Joshua doesn't like them, and really, no one likes them, so I think everyone should just leave them alone. Allah will take care of it." I didn't usually talk to Toni about Allah, but she understood that I was serious when I did.

"You got it, Lou. It's your call, and *I ain't like bein' roun' them no how*," Toni said in her worst grammar and most Southern drawl. "*Let's tell Joshua so he don't have to deal with their sorry selves neither*." Did I mention that I love her?

Nabbed!

I let Miranda and Robbie know that we aborted the mission, and that should have been the end of it, but it wasn't. Toni was on her way outside to meet us after she told Joshua, but the Veries hunted her down on the way out. Toni tried to lose them in her polite way, but they didn't take the message. They followed her to the playground where Robbie, Miranda and I were having a swinging contest on the jungle gym, and we heard Very B. yelling at Toni, "Come on back! We have something to show you!"

"No thank you, I'll catch y'all later," Toni called back on her way over to us, but the Veries were just not going to let her go without a fight.

"Come on, Toni, you need to see this!" Toni stopped in her tracks, turned around and started to walk towards them. I figured she was going to tell them to buzz off, but instead, she went back with them inside. Miranda, Robbie and I went in behind them, quietly. Miranda took off her clicky shoes once we were inside so they wouldn't hear us. We stopped around the corner from the bathroom that Toni and the Veries entered. After a minute, I was considering going in after Toni to save her, but Robbie held me back. Good thing she did, because Hoops went into the bathroom a minute later and came out with Ms. Matthews, Toni and the Veries! *Oh, snap! Toni is in trouble and it's all my fault!*

Alhamdulillah, Toni wasn't in trouble, though. *Phew!* She turned around towards us and Ms. Matthews and Hoops marched the Veries towards the office. As soon as they turned the corner, Toni ran towards us smiling and said, "I knew y'all would follow me inside."

"What happened?" Miranda asked, while we headed out to the playground.

"The Veries had another bag of ink, and the teachers caught them talking about it," Toni answered, trying not to speak too loudly.

"Oh. My. Word. How did they know?" Miranda asked.

"Yeah, how did they know? We aborted the plan!" I said.

"Yes, we did, but they didn't," Toni said. "After we talked in the bathroom earlier, I went to tell Joshua that we were aborting, and he told me that the Veries had already told him that they had a bag of ink in the bathroom. They planned on getting Robbie on the bus home today, *plus,* they were going to set you up to take the fall. So I lured them outside while Joshua went and told Hoops. And that's all she wrote!"

"Toni! Alhamdulillah, you're my hero!" I screamed, hugging her. She looked really embarrassed and opened her mouth to redefine our relationship again, but Miranda and Robbie laughed and hugged her. So she just took all the hugs and started laughing, too.

The Veries weren't on the bus on the way home. I should have been happy that they were gone, but I was a little bit sad, and I didn't know exactly why. But I finally had the chance to tell my friends about the kittens, and Toni was going to come over after band practice and homework. Robbie and Miranda were going to ask their parents if they could have a kitten. If they could, then none of the kittens would have to go to the shelter, insha Allah. Miss Abigail already had two dogs, a cat and a lizard, so Toni was pretty sure she would not be able to take one.

When I got home, I yelled "Asalaam alaikum!" and saw there was a brand new book bag, with new notebooks, pencils, markers, pencil case, lanyard, cell phone case, journal, calculator and lunch box sitting in the middle of the living room floor. *Cool!* They *had* to be for me, because, well, they just had to be. "Mama! Where are you? What's this stuff?"

Mama came out of the kitchen with a cheery pie and put it on the dining table and said, "Wa alaikum asalaam, Lulubug. Do you like your new school supplies?"

"Oh, I love them, *jazak Allahu khair*, Mama! But just wait. I need to tell you what happened today. And Mo and Sho, too, and Baba. It was um, a very interesting day."

"Alright, go say 'salaam' to the kittens and then go make wudu. Your Baba will be home in a few minutes, and we can pray, eat an early dinner, and talk about your very interesting day at school," Mama answered.

"What's for dinner? I'm hungrier than the kittens!" I said, watching them chomp down on their food mix. Alhamdulillah, they looked healthy, and Cutie Brown had wet paws and face from diving head first into the water dish. He was so adorable! I think I loved him the best, even though they were all very lovable. I snuggled each kitten for a few minutes and then went to make wudu.

When Baba and my brothers came home, we prayed and then set the table to eat. Mama had made my favorite– *pâtes au gratin*, which sounds like "patso-gratton, and is just a fancy schmancy French way of saying macaroni and cheese. We also had turkey ham and yummy cauliflower, with cheery pie for dessert. One of Mama's best meals EVER, alhamdulillah. *Baba Ganoogie!*

I told my family everything that went on at school, including the Veries getting nabbed by Hoops and Ms. Matthews. They all agreed with me that it was good to catch them in the act, but it was kind of sad that people felt like they had to be so mean. They understood when I said I wasn't as happy on the bus as I should have been. They also agreed, Mo and Sho too, that maybe working under a bunch of lies might not be the best way to solve a problem, and that sometimes, things just need to be left to Allah.

Sho asked about my new school supplies and I said, "Mama got them for me today, alhamdulillah."

"That's not quite correct, Habibti," Baba said. "But let your Mama tell you."

"Well," Mama said, "I had a little talk with the Veronicas' parents this morning."

"Mama! What did you say?" I asked. As I said, Mama knows how to take care of business.

"Habibti, I'm not going to tell you what I said, but let's just say I used my powers of persuasion, with a little bit of sweetness, effectively," Mama said, and winked. I'm glad that Mama is on my team. I wouldn't want to be her enemy, even if she was bringing cheery pie to my doorstep.

"Come on, Mom, can't you tell us a little bit?" Sho asked, but Mama shook her head, and Baba laughed. Some things just will have to remain a mystery.

After dinner, I went upstairs with my new school supplies to do my homework. Since Toni was going to come over to see the kittens, I got cracking on it right away. It didn't take me long to finish and Toni still hadn't come over, so I looked out my bedroom window with the binoculars and got a little sad. I was really going to miss my woods and my hometown, and especially my friends, and especially Toni.

I turned on my computer because it would be nice to talk to my cousin Michaela, but Ducky was probably in bed, because there is a big time difference between the United States and Egypt. Michaela wasn't online, but hey, Moby was! I hadn't talked to her since Saturday when Mama and I went to the masjid. It seemed like a million years ago, and I really did want to talk to her. She seemed like a very nice person, that is, after she knocked me on my bum. It would be nice, and useful, to have a friend in my new school before I start.

"Asalaam alaikum, Moby!" I said.

"Wa alaikum asalaam, Lou!" Moby answered. "Hey, I'm glad you're online. My mother wanted to talk to your mom for a minute."

"Why, whassup?" I asked.

"She wants to invite your family to my big sister's wedding next month."

"Way cool! Let me get her!" I ran downstairs with my laptop.

Mama and Moby's mother started talking, and stayed on FOREVER. Mama sure can talk when she feels like it, so Moby called my cell phone, and she told me a little about the wedding. Moby's sister's name is Lina, and she studies biology at the university. Her fiancé's name is Kareem, and he studies business. Moby said that the wedding was going to be interesting, even if it wasn't fun, because not all the family members like each other. Hmm. I wouldn't know a fun wedding from an interesting wedding, because I've never been to either. So it will certainly be an educational wedding, if nothing else.

Moby and I got off the phone because of the asr azhan. After praying, Toni and I played with the kittens, and I was happy. Alhamdulillah for what He gave me in friends and family and Cutie Brown. Life was good, alhamdulillah.

Mac McGooshie

~The End~

<u>Lulubug's Personal Dictionary</u>

Ala mode– Fancy schmancy French words that mean "with ice cream on top."

Alhamdulillah– Arabic word that every Muslim uses to thank God, Allah, for everything. It means "All praises are for Allah."

Allah, subhanna wa ta'ala– Allah is the Creator of the heavens and the earth and all that lies between them. Allah made everything that is, and everything that happened, and everything that will happen. "Subhanna wa ta'ala" is what Muslims say when we're talking about Allah, which means "Glorified and Almighty." This is a big deal.

Amitoo– Arabic word that means "Auntie on Baba's side."

Asalaam alaikum– Arabic words that sorta mean "Blessings and Mercy of Allah to you." Muslims say "Asalaam alaikum" instead of "Hey, whassup?"

Audhu billah min shaytan ar-rajeem– that's what Muslims say when we want to protect ourselves from Shaytan, or from very bad stuff. Sometimes people get scared for no good reason, and it helps to say this.

Azhan– this is Muslims' call to prayer that happens every day, five times a day.

Bismillah Ar-Rahman Ar-Raheem – This is Arabic for "In the name of Allah, the Most Gracious, the Most Merciful." Muslims use this sentence, and sometimes just "Bismillah" when they start to do something good, like get out of the bed in the morning.

Chandelier pretty, glassy, lights that hang from the ceiling.

De facto disaster area– means that you can call it whatever you want, it looks like a disaster area and will be treated as such.

Deen– Arabic word that means "religion."

Devastated – super sad, which is how I felt when my favorite TV show about the monkeys went off the air.

Duaa– this is a little prayer to Allah when we want to ask for something.

Five times for a Muslim's prayer– 1) *Fajr*- at dawn, before the sun comes up– 2) *Zhur*- just after noon– 3) *Asr*- in the later afternoon– 4) *Maghrib*- after the sun goes down, but before it's completely dark – 5) *Isha*-After there is no light from the sun at all.

Habibi (for a boy or a girl) and **Habibti** (for a girl)– Arabic words that mean "my love" or "my darling."

Halal –Arabic word that means "permitted." No problem, Pedro.

Haram– Arabic word that means "forbidden." No way, Jose.

Inna lillahi wa inna lillahi rajioon– This is Arabic for "Surely we belong to Allah and surely to Him will we return." This is what Muslims say when someone dies. It is a reminder that Allah is the One who created us and will take us at any time. Just a reminder.

Insha Allah– Arabic words that mean "if Allah lets." Muslims say this when we plan on doing something.

Jannah– Paradise. It's where good people go after Judgment Day, if Allah lets.

Jazak Allahu khair- means "May Allah reward you with goodness." Muslims say this instead of "thanks very much." (If you haven't noticed, Muslims think about Allah a lot!)

Jihad– Arabic word that means "struggle." Muslims sometimes use the word to describe when they have to go to war, but mostly they talk about things they have to work on to make themselves better people. Like learning to be more patient. Or being nice to people you just don't like.

Jumaah– Arabic word for "Friday" and my favorite day of the week.

Kosher– this is a Jewish word that means "halal," and this is okay for Muslims (and Jews) to eat.

La ilaha il-Allah! Mohammed ar-Rasoul Allah! – This is Arabic, which means "There is no god but Allah! Mohamed is the Messenger of Allah!"

Laughing hyena– an animal found in Africa that looks like a wild dog. It makes laughing noises (but it's not really laughing) to communicate with the other hyenas in its clan.

Ma'alish– an Egyptian expression that Mama doesn't like which means "Never mind," or "Fuggetaboutit."

Masha Allah– Arabic expression that mean "With Allah's will." Or in other words, "Because Allah let it happen." Muslims believe that everything that happens, whether we like it or we don't, happens because Allah said so.

Masjid– this is the building where Muslims go to pray.

Monsoon– a super huge rain storm that (usually) takes place in south Asia.

Musalla– the prayer room for Muslims.

Muslim– a person who believes that there is no god but Allah and that Mohamed is the prophet and messenger of Allah. Only one Allah!

Pollination– This is what happens when pollen from one flower is moved to another flower. Pollination is necessary for many flowering plants to grow and make food. Bees are most excellent pollinators!

Presumption of culpability– means that you will have to work pretty darned hard to prove that you are innocent.

Prophet Mohamed, sallallahu alaihi wa salaam- This wonderful man is the man that Allah used to establish Islam on earth, after Prophet Jesus (alaihi wa salaam), who was another wonderful man. Muslims love all the prophets of Allah, and especially Prophet Mohamed because he is Islam's prophet.

Psyche– a fancy schmancy way of talking about a person's mental state. Shocking someone's psyche is very impolite, usually.

Quran– the holy book of Islam. It's the rule book for Muslims.

Rhetorical– a fancy way of extra talking that does not mean anything. Mama says "One does not answer rhetorical questions unless one wishes to get into trouble."

Sabr– Arabic word that means "patience."

Sadaqa– Arabic word meaning "charity." Muslims like to do charitable work because it makes Allah happy. Ka-Ching!

Sasquatch– AKA Bigfoot. He's a big, hairy guy who is supposed to live in the woods. But he doesn't exist. Really. Except in my imagination.

Second Amendment– This is the amendment to the United States Constitution that states that people have the right to own guns– big guns, small guns, medium guns. Does not refer to a child's right to own a slingshot, paint gun, or crossbow, Mama says.

Sister– not just sharing DNA! Muslims are all part of one big family, called the "Ummah." Muslims call each other brother and sister, even if one Muslim is from India, another one from Nigeria, another one from Germany, another one from Jupiter, and so on and so forth.

Sitoo– Arabic word meaning "Grandmother."

Stepford wife– a robot woman who cannot think for herself and does anything her husband tells her without thinking whether it's good or bad. Mama says that's just crazy.

Subhan Allah!– Means "Glory to Allah!" Muslims say this when we are floored by the things we see, like a beautiful flower, a cute kitten, or a raging thunderstorm.

Surah– a chapter in the Quran

Surgeon– a doctor who opens a body to fix it. Very tricky, surgeons are.

Tutu– Hawaiian word meaning "Grandmother."

Vindication– fancy schmancy word that means "I didn't do it, and here is my proof!"

Wa alaikum asalaam– Arabic words that sorta mean "Mercy and blessings of Allah to you, too." See "asalaam alaikum." Muslims say "wa alaikum asalaam" instead of "Not much, whassup with you?"

Wudu– cleaning for prayers, which means washing the hands, mouth, nose, face, arms, head, ears and feet.

Lulu and the Very Big Meanies

Mac McGooshie

Coming soon, insha Allah

Lulu
and the
Monkey
Marriage

#2 in Lulubug's Week in the Life Series

CPSIA information can be obtained
at www.ICGtesting.com
Printed in the USA
BVHW03s0014300418
514756BV00023B/195/P

9 780985 463823